The Green Team
The Adventures of Mitch and Molly

Karen O'Connor

Illustrated by Len Ebert

CONCORDIA®
PUBLISHING HOUSE

The Adventures of Mitch and Molly

The Green Team
The Water Detectives

———— *The Green Team* is printed on recycled paper. ————

Library of Congress Cataloging-in-Publication Data

O'Conner, Karen, 1938–
     The Green Team the adventures of Mitch and Molly / Karen O'Connor; illustrated by Len Ebert.
(God's green earth; bk. 1)
Summary: Concerned about helping take better care of God's planet, Mitch and Molly rescue a seagull caught in a plastic six-pack ring.
ISBN 0-570-04726-9
     [1. Wildlife rescue—Fiction. 2. Environmental protection—Fiction. 3. Gulls—Fiction. 4. Christian life—Fiction. 5. Brothers and sisters—Fiction.] I. Ebert, Len , ill. II. Title. III. Series.

PZ7.02224Gr   1993   [E]—dc20   92-24643
                                                            CIP

1 2 3 4 5 6 7 8 9 10   02 01 00 99 98 97 96 95 94 93

★
For Noah and Johannah
(The real Mitch and Molly in my life)

Contents

Mitch and Molly
And the Green Team

Mitch ran all the way home from school. He was out of breath when he burst through the front door. "Grandma, Molly," he shouted. "Guess what? I'm going to be on the Green Team."

Grandma walked into the family room and gave Mitch a hug. Molly sat in the brown chair, brushing her cat, Fluffy. "That sounds exciting," said Grandma. "Tell me more."

Mitch gulped down the apple juice Grandma poured. "Mayor Price wants every school in the city to make a garden," said Mitch. "Everyone who helps will be on the mayor's Green Team. We even get a certificate with our name on it. And the school with the prettiest garden gets a special award."

Mitch grabbed an oatmeal cookie. "The kids at the winning school get to go on a field trip to a big garden," said Mitch.

"Is it Harrington Gardens?" asked Grandma, smiling.

"That's it. How did you know, Grandma?"

"Well I've been there. It's a very beautiful place."

"We saw it on a video," said Mitch. "The man on the video talked about how plants help us. He said plants and people are partners. Plants breathe out oxygen. That's what people need to breathe in. And people breathe out carbon dioxide. Plants take in carbon dioxide. They keep the air clean and pure," said Mitch. "Isn't that cool, Grandma?"

"It certainly is. That's why I have so many plants at home," said Grandma.

"Wow! I didn't know that," said Mitch. "I

want a plant in my room."

Molly looked up from brushing Fluffy. "Can I be on the Green Team too?" she asked.

"Sorry, Molly. It's just for kids who are 8 to 12 years old. But you can help me if you want."

Molly frowned. "Can I have a plant in my room?"

"That's a good idea," said Grandma. "Let's talk to your mother about it when she comes home."

Suddenly Mitch jumped up and looked at the clock. It was ten minutes after four. "Grandma, we have to hurry. Tomorrow is the last day to join. I was sick last week so I didn't know till today. We have to go to the nursery right now," Mitch said, tugging on Grandma's sleeve.

"Slow down, Mitch. Tell me what you need."

"Each person who wants to be on the team has to bring a plant for the garden. We can buy one at Green Gardens," said Mitch.

"We can't do that today," said Grandma. "Your mother and dad have the car, remember?"

Mitch plopped down on the floor. He had forgotten that his parents had taken the car on their trip. Mitch watched Grandma rest her chin in her hands. He knew she was thinking hard.

Suddenly Grandma looked up. "They'll be home in two days," she said. "You can get a plant then. I'll write a note to your teacher. I'm sure she will understand."

"No, no, Grandma," said Mitch, jumping up and down. "Tomorrow is the last day. If we don't bring a plant tomorrow we don't get a certificate."

Mitch sat down next to Grandma. "Mayor Price said everyone had to keep the same rules or they couldn't be in the contest."

"Well Mitch, we'll have to think about this," said Grandma. "Let's say a little prayer. I'm sure the Lord will show us what to do."

Grandma took Mitch and Molly by the hand. "Dear Lord," she said. "You know Mitch wants to be on the Green Team. Please show us what to do. Amen."

"We know you can help us," said Mitch. "Amen."

"Amen," said Molly.

Mitch and Molly set the table for dinner while Grandma made some hot soup and banana bread. But Mitch couldn't stop looking at the clock. He wished God would hurry up and give him an answer. Pretty soon it would be too late to buy a plant. Green Gardens would be closed after dinner.

Mitch felt sad. He didn't see how he could be on the team. There was no way to get to the nursery on time.

After dinner Grandma wrapped up a loaf of banana bread. "Mitch, would you please take this to Mrs. Bell? She's all alone, and I think this will cheer her up."

Mitch hung his head. He didn't feel like

visiting their next door neighbor. All he could think of was the contest and the Green Team and the school garden. But he said, "Sure, Grandma."

"You don't sound too happy about it."

"I can't stop thinking about the Green Team," said Mitch.

"Hang on," said Grandma. "The Lord knows what you need."

"Then why doesn't He give it to me?" asked Mitch.

"Well, I guess it's not time yet," said Grandma.

Mitch didn't understand how Grandma could be so calm. His stomach was jumping up and down inside.

Grandma wrapped the banana bread. Mitch tied a red ribbon around it. Then he walked over to Mrs. Bell's house.

Mitch could see her peeking through the curtains. She opened the door even before he knocked. "What a nice surprise," said Mrs.

Bell. "Is that for me?"

"It's from Grandma," said Mitch. "She said it might cheer you up."

"Well, tell her I feel cheered up just looking at it. And what a lovely ribbon."

Mitch smiled for the first time all evening. "I put that on," he said.

"Can you visit for a few minutes?" asked Mrs. Bell. "I hardly see you and Molly anymore now that you're in school all day. What are you studying?"

Mitch began talking about the Green Team and the contest and the school garden. Then he told her about the video he saw. "Mrs. Bell, did you know that people and plants are partners?"

"Why, yes I do," she said. "Just look at all my plants. They take a lot of time, but I don't mind. They're like friends."

Mitch had never thought about plants being friends. But as Mrs. Bell talked he could see she was right. "Friends do nice things for each other," she said. "I water them and give them a place to grow. And they fill up my house with clean air and pretty smells and colors."

She's right, thought Mitch. Plants are like friends. He thought how nice it was to sit under a shady tree on a hot day. And he remembered the beautiful purple and white flowers at the park. He thought about the grassy field at church where the kids played. And he remembered the tall shrubs that made a fence around their yard.

Mrs. Bell sure knows a lot about plants, thought Mitch. She's like a walking garden book. Then he laughed to himself, imagining a book with arms and legs and a head. Mitch was having so much fun with Mrs. Bell that he didn't feel sick inside anymore. And he wasn't worried about the contest and the Green Team.

"Mitch." Mrs. Bell leaned forward in her chair. Mitch sat up straight. "You seem very interested in plants," she said. "I wonder if you could help me out." Mrs. Bell walked over to the patio door. Mitch noticed that her pink dress matched the flowers in the little vase on the table. "I have so many plants," she said. "I'd like to give you and Molly some to take care of."

"You would? You mean it?" Mitch could hardly believe it. He followed Mrs. Bell out to her garden. Mrs. Bell was going to *give* him some plants.

"Thanks a lot, Mrs. Bell. That sure is nice of you."

"That's what friends are for," she said with a twinkle in her eye. "Friends share what they have with each other."

Mrs. Bell smiled as she gave Mitch a tray with three small pots. She pointed to the one with the bright red flowers. "This is a geranium plant," she said. "And the one next to it is a marigold. It's almost ready to bloom."

Then Mrs. Bell handed Mitch a small blue pot. "And these are called snapdragons. They get pretty tall. So be sure to plant them in an outdoor garden," she said.

Mitch could hardly stand still. She said to plant them outside. The school garden. That's it, thought Mitch. Here was the plant he needed. He could be on the Green Team after all. He would get a certificate. His school might get the award, and he might go on the field trip. And he and Molly would each have a plant for their rooms.

"Thanks, Mrs. Bell," said Mitch, as he waved good-bye. "Thanks a lot."

"I'm glad you came to visit, Mitch. And tell your grandma thank you for the banana bread."

Mitch took a deep breath. He whispered a little prayer. Then he pushed open the front door and ran through the house. "Grandma, Molly! Come quick," he called. "Wait till you hear how God answered our prayers."

SOMETHING YOU CAN DO TO SAVE GOD'S GREEN EARTH

Plant some flowers in your yard or in a window garden. Water them and give them flower food each week. Read about your flowers in a gardening book or in an encyclopedia.

Show your teacher this story. Ask him or her to organize a Green Team at your school or in your classroom. You may be able to get the whole school involved in a tree-planting program.

Mitch and Molly
And the Stranded Sea Gull

Mitch pulled his sister by the hand. "Hurry, Molly!" he called. "There's the ocean. Last one in is a rotten egg." Mitch dashed through the sand and jumped into the water. His light-blue swimming trunks turned dark blue as the cold water hit him.

Molly dug her toes into the wet sand. "It's fre-e-e-zing," she said. "I want Mommy to come with me."

"She's watching us. She's right there with Grandpa under the yellow and white umbrella," said Mitch.

Mitch and Molly waved. Mother and

Grandpa waved back.

"Watch me, Molly," he shouted. "I can do the dead-man's float."

"Good, Mitch. Now let's collect shells," said Molly.

Mitch ran along the shore with his sister. "I found one," he shouted, holding up a pretty white shell with brown stripes.

"Me too," said Molly.

"I wish the whole beach was as pretty as these shells," Mitch said. "Look at all this trash. Bags and cups and cans are all over the place. The fish and birds could get sick if they eat that stuff. I wish we could do something to help."

Mitch sat down and played with a stick in the sand. He remembered what he learned in vacation Bible school. It was about being a good steward. His class had made a big mural for the back wall. They called it "God's Green Earth." Each boy and girl had painted a picture of one of God's creatures. Mitch thought about the sea gull he drew.

Molly plopped down on the sand next to Mitch. "Don't you want to look for shells anymore?"

Mitch looked up. "Sure. I was just thinking about what Mr. Morgan said in vacation Bible school. He said if everyone was a good steward the earth would be a nice place for all God's creatures."

"What's a steward?" asked Molly.

Mitch almost got mad at Molly for not knowing the answer. Then he remembered that she was only five.

Mitch dug a hole in the wet sand. "A steward is someone who takes care of things," he said.

"Like a baby-sitter?" asked Molly. "Jennifer takes care of us when Mommy and Daddy go out for dinner. Is she a steward?"

"Yeah, kind of," said Mitch. He made a little castle out of wet sand. "God's stewards take care of His creatures. Like plants and animals and stuff like that."

Molly patted the sand castle. "When I give Fluffy clean water and food, is that being a steward?" she asked.

"Yeah, that's right," said Mitch. "Remember when you and Daddy made her a scratching post? That was being a steward too." Mitch stood up and watched the little birds on the shore. "Mr. Morgan said we're good stewards when we throw away our trash after a picnic. And when we pick up cans and cups on the beach." Mitch dug a tunnel around the castle.

He felt very grown-up telling Molly about being a steward. Then suddenly Mitch felt sad. He looked around at all the trash. Some people aren't good stewards, he thought.

"Caw! Caw!"

"What is that funny noise?" Molly asked. Mitch looked up. Sea gulls flapped their wings. He remembered how last year one sea gull had eaten a piece of bread right out of his hand.

"Time for lunch!" Mitch heard his mother call. He and Molly ran to the red towel under the big umbrella. Mother passed out plates and cups. Grandpa poured the lemonade, and Molly opened a bowl of potato salad. Mother and Mitch and Molly and Grandpa held hands.

"Thank You, Lord, for this food," said Mother.

"And thank You for my family," said Grandpa.

"And for the pretty shells," added Molly.

"And thank You for the sea gulls," said Mitch. "Amen."

"That's a fine castle you made," said Grandpa, as he sipped his lemonade. "What else have you two been up to?"

"We collected these shells," said Molly. "This pink one is my favorite."

"And I did the dead-man's float," said Mitch.

"Well," said Grandpa, "that calls for a celebration. How about some cold watermelon when we get back to the cottage?" he asked.

Suddenly a flock of noisy sea gulls swooped down and landed near the umbrella. "Caw! Caw!" One bird walked toward Mitch. The gull flapped its wings and opened its beak.

"They look hungry," Mitch said. "Can we feed them?"

"Oh, please," said Molly.

"Of course," said Mother. "I brought along some bread crumbs just for the birds." She opened a bag, and Mitch and Molly and Grandpa each grabbed a handful.

Mitch threw some of the bread on the sand. Molly tossed a piece over her head. One bird swooped down and caught it in mid-air! Mitch saw another gull standing away from the others. It had something strange hanging around its neck. Mitch got down on his hands and knees to get a closer look.

"Mommy, Grandpa," shouted Mitch. "That bird needs help. It has a plastic ring around its neck."

Mother crawled out from under the umbrella. Grandpa leaned forward in his beach chair. Molly sat very still and stared at the bird.

"We must tell someone," said Mother. "It looks like a plastic ring, the kind that's around canned drinks."

Grandpa looked worried. "The bird might die if we don't get help," he said quietly.

Molly grabbed Grandpa's hand. "I'm scared," she said. "I don't want it to die."

"There's a lifeguard station," shouted Mitch.

"Good," said Mother. "Let's talk to someone there."

Mitch could feel his heart pounding. He and Mother walked over to the lifeguard station. "Dear God," Mitch whispered, "help us save that bird."

A lady with blonde hair stepped outside. "Hi! My name is Judy," she said, smiling. "What can I do for you?"

"I'm Mitch, and this is my mom. There's a

sea gull with a plastic ring around its neck. If we don't help it, it might die," said Mitch all in one breath. He talked so fast he wasn't sure if all the words came out right.

"This sounds serious," said Judy. "Thank you for telling me. Let's see what we can do. We'll need a scissors and a towel."

"We have a towel," said Mitch.

"Good! And I have a scissors in my bag," said Judy.

"Grandpa and I will wait under the umbrella," said Mother. "You go with Judy, Mitch and Molly. Too many people might frighten the bird."

Mitch and Molly followed Judy over to the sea gull. "We don't want to scare it off," she said. "We must walk slowly and be very quiet." When Judy got close to the bird, she knelt down. Then she slowly opened the towel and quickly threw it over the bird.

Gently, she picked up the frightened creature. "Caw! Caw!" squawked the other birds.

Mitch knew they were afraid too.

"We won't hurt you," Judy whispered.

"We want to help you," said Mitch.

Judy carefully unwrapped the bird. She took her scissors and snipped the plastic ring from its neck. Then she set it down on the sand. Mitch pulled out some bread crumbs from his pocket. He threw them on the sand. The gull gobbled them up. Then it flapped its wings and flew off.

Judy smiled at Mitch. "You saved that bird's life," she said. Mitch felt warm and happy inside. Mother and Grandpa were standing up next to the umbrella. They looked happy too. Judy walked back to the umbrella with Mitch and Molly. She sat down and Mother poured everyone a cup of lemonade. Then she passed out the apple-nut cookies that Molly and Grandpa had made.

"Thousands of fish and birds die every year," said Judy. "People leave their plastic trash on the beach and in the parks." She pointed at the ocean. "Look at the porpoises jumping," she said. "Porpoises and dolphins and turtles are endangered animals for the same reason—plastic trash."

Judy sipped her lemonade and bit into a cookie. "These sea animals swim into six-pack rings like the one on the sea gull we helped. Some choke on plastic bags and on cups that float on the water. I wish more people picked up their trash," said Judy.

"Wow!" Mitch could hardly believe it. He was surprised that so many fish and birds die because people are careless. "We need to take care of the beach and the park," said Mitch.

"You're right," said Mother. "The animals need people who care about them. God wants all His creatures to have a good life."

"How can we help?" asked Mitch.

"Can I help too?" asked Molly.

"You sure can," said Judy. "You can make a big difference. You can start today. Come with me. I have a list of things you can do to clean up the beach."

Judy, Mitch and Molly, and Mother and Grandpa walked over to the lifeguard station. Judy handed Mitch a piece of paper. At the top it said, "Be a Beach Buddy." Mitch showed the list to Mother and Molly and Grandpa. Mother read it out loud.

Be a Beach Buddy

1. Take a large trash bag with you when you visit the beach or park.

2. Pick up soda cans and smash them. Put them in your bag.

3. Pick up plastic six-pack rings. Snip each ring with a scissors. Put the rings in the trash bag so birds and fish will not be hurt.

4. Avoid Styrofoam containers. They are dangerous to sea animals. Styrofoam pellets look like food to fish and birds. If they eat them, they can die. If you see Styrofoam on the beach or in the park, put it in your trash bag. Use hard plastic, or paper plates and cups for your picnic lunch.

5. Put all of your garbage in your bag or in a trash container. Don't leave anything behind.

Mother handed the paper to Mitch. "We could do all these things," he said. "Our friends could help us."

"That's right," Judy said. "If everyone did a little bit, we could keep our parks and beaches clean. And we would save the animals, birds, and fish too."

Judy smiled. "I have to go back to the station," she said. "But if you'd like to get started, come by my office. I'll give you a trash bag."

Mitch and Molly picked up a bag from Judy. Then they ran back to Mother and Grandpa. They walked along the beach together. Grandpa carried the trash bag. Mitch put aluminum cans in the bag. Mother picked up some plastic cups. Molly found two six-pack rings. Grandpa grabbed some paper sacks blowing across the sand. When the bag was full, Mitch twisted the top closed. He dropped it in the trash can.

Then Mitch and Molly and Mother and

Grandpa picked up their towel, umbrella, and picnic basket. They walked back to their car.

"We had a good day, didn't we?" asked Mother.

"I had fun, and I learned a lot too," said Mitch.

"Me too," said Molly. "I learned what a steward is. Mitch is a steward," she said proudly. "He saved a sea gull."

"Why, that's right," said Grandpa. "Mighty smart of you to notice, young lady," he said, and winked at Molly. Then Grandpa cleared his throat and said, "Mitch, this calls for a celebration. What do you say we change that to *two* slices of watermelon?"

"Wow, thanks, Grandpa."

As Mitch opened the car door he heard a familiar sound. "Caw! Caw!" He looked up. A big sea gull flapped its wings and flew through the sky. Mitch felt warm and happy inside. He whispered a little prayer. "Thank You, God, for sea gulls."

SOMETHING YOU CAN DO TO SAVE GOD'S GREEN EARTH

Make a flier like the one Judy gave to Mitch and Molly. Ask your parents and teachers at school and Sunday school if you can help organize a field trip. You could go to the woods or the beach or park to clean up the trash. Here are some names you could use for your flier:

BE A BEACH BUDDY

BE A FOREST FRIEND

BE A PARK PAL

Mitch and Molly
And the Backyard Visitors

Mitch poked at the peas on his dinner plate. He made a little circle with his fork in the mashed potatoes.

"You seem unhappy," said Mitch's dad. "Do you want to talk about it?"

"Louis took my idea for the science fair," said Mitch, frowning. "I told him I was going to show the kids how to grow a flower. But he signed up for it today while I was in the bathroom." Mitch looked at the packet of flower seeds on the kitchen shelf. "Grandpa even gave me the marigold seeds, remember?"

"I remember," said Dad. "And I remember

the note you brought home from school. God's Green Earth Third Grade Science Fair, right?"

"Right," said Mitch. "Each person gets to do one experiment about plants. We're going to show them on Parents' Night."

"Did you tell your teacher what happened with Louis?" asked Dad.

"I tried to," said Mitch, "but Mr. Bond said he couldn't be sure who was telling the truth. He said whoever signed up first could do that project. Louis lied, Dad. He said he had the idea before me, but he didn't." Mitch gulped his milk and took a small bite of chicken.

"It's not fair," said Mitch. "I need an idea right now. Tomorrow is the last day to sign up."

Mitch's father sipped his iced tea. "I'm sorry you had so much trouble," he said. "It hurts when a friend tells a lie."

Mother reached for the hot rolls. "I'm sorry too," she said. "But I know you'll find a new idea. Maybe it will be even better than the old one." Mother winked at Mitch. "Don't forget to ask the Lord what He thinks," she said, smiling. "And trust Him to help Louis learn to tell the truth."

"Hey, Mitch. Guess what?" Molly interrupted. She smiled at him through her milk mustache. "Rachel has some red flowers in her yard. They're called honeysuckle." Molly wrinkled her nose and laughed. "Isn't that a funny name? And now two hummingbirds are in her yard every day. Rachel's mom said honeysuckle is their favorite flower—especially red ones."

"Gosh, Molly, do you have to talk *all* the time? I don't care about Rachel and the hummingbirds," Mitch said in a loud voice. "I'm trying to think of a science project, okay?"

Molly ran from the kitchen crying. Mitch knew he had hurt her feelings.

Dad turned to Mitch with a serious look on his face. Mitch knew he was in big trouble. "That was wrong," said Dad. "Molly was sharing something important to her."

"I'm sorry, Dad, but she talks too much. I'm trying to think of what to do for the science fair. She interrupted me."

"Maybe so," said Dad, "but that doesn't make it all right for you to be rude."

"How about if Mother and I do the dishes tonight?" asked Dad. "You can go upstairs and think about what you did to Molly. And you can work on the science fair too. Maybe Molly can help you."

Mitch made a face when Dad wasn't looking. He liked not having to do the dishes. But he sure didn't want a little kid helping him with the science fair. Molly doesn't know anything about science, thought Mitch. She's just a kindergartner. All they do is play with clay and sing songs.

Mitch ran upstairs. When he got to Molly's room, he stopped. The door was closed. I'll tell her I'm sorry in the morning, thought Mitch. But he knew he wouldn't be able to sleep if he didn't talk to her now. Mitch's heart pounded hard. He took a deep breath and knocked on the door. "Molly, it's me, Mitch."

"What do you want?" called Molly.

"I-I'm sorry for yelling at you," said Mitch.

Molly opened the door. She was smiling. Now Mitch felt even worse. He knew his little sister loved him. He felt all soft inside. He loved her too. And he knew he should be nicer to her.

"Okay, Molly, you can help me think of an idea for the science fair. But it has to be a really good one," he said, "even better than Louis', okay?"

"Sure," said Molly. "But first can I finish telling you about Rachel?"

Mitch felt angry again. He just told Molly he didn't want to hear about Rachel.

"All right. You can tell me one more thing, but that's all," said Mitch.

Molly twisted the bottom of her T-shirt. "Well," she said, "Rachel's mom said they're going to make their backyard into a wildlife habitat."

"What does that mean?" asked Mitch in a mean voice.

"It means a place for wild animals to live," said Molly.

Mitch laughed out loud. Then he jumped up and down and made funny faces and strange noises. "Wild animals, Molly? Like lions and tigers and bears? Nobody has wild animals in their backyard. You have to go to the zoo and the circus to see wild animals," he said proudly.

Molly stamped her foot and put her hands on her hips. "No you don't," she said. "There are lots of wild animals and birds all around. Rachel's dad said butterflies and humming-birds and moths and squirrels and rabbits are wildlife. And he knows, 'cause he's a park ranger."

"Okay," said Mitch. "Are you finished now?"

"No, I'm not," said Molly. "You said I

could tell you one more thing about Rachel's yard. And I'm not finished yet."

Mitch knew he better listen, or Dad would be upset. "Okay, Molly, but hurry up. You're taking too long. I have to work on the science fair."

Molly took a deep breath. "Okay, I'll talk fast," she said. "Rachel's family is going to plant pretty flowers so butterflies will come. They're building a hummingbird feeder too. And Rachel's dad is putting a pile of wood by the back fence. He said a woodchuck or a squirrel might make a nest there."

Molly plopped down on her bed. "Did you know rabbits and squirrels, and even deer, used to live around here before all these houses were built?"

Mitch didn't know that. But he pretended he did. "Of course. Everyone knows that," said Mitch. "This whole neighborhood had lots of birds and butterflies and . . . "

Mitch stopped. He couldn't think of anything more to say. Molly had a funny look on her face, like she didn't believe him. Mitch got a pain in his stomach. He wondered if pretending was like telling a lie.

Lying made Mitch think about Louis again. And when he thought of Louis he started thinking about the science fair.

"Okay, Molly. That's enough. I have to work on the science fair. And you're not helping. I don't have time for any more about Rachel."

Molly slid off her bed. She smoothed out the wrinkles on the bedspread. "Bye, Mitch," she said. "I hope you get a good idea for the science fair."

"Thanks, Molly."

Mitch went to his room, put his head down, and closed his eyes. He still felt kind of sick in his stomach. He knew he had lied to Molly, just like Louis had lied to Mr. Bond. Mitch felt mixed up inside. He didn't know what to do.

Then he remembered that Mom had told

him to ask God about the science fair. And he thought about how Dad said he never made an important decision without praying first.

Mitch wondered if God would even listen to him, since he had told a lie.

He decided to try. "God, I feel terrible," said Mitch. "I got mad at Molly. Then I told her a lie. I'm so sorry. And now my stomach feels sick. And I have to think of a good idea for the science fair. Please help me. Thanks. Amen."

Mitch always felt better after he prayed. But sometimes it was hard to wait for an answer. He decided he should tell Molly he was sorry for lying. He would do that first.

"Molly," Mitch called. "Can you come here for a second? I have to tell you something really important."

"Here I come," said Molly. Fluffy meowed. She followed Molly into Mitch's room and jumped up on his bed. "What do you want?" asked Molly.

Mitch felt so nervous he could hardly talk.

"Molly, remember when I told you I knew about the wildlife in our neighborhood?" Molly shook her head up and down. "Well, I didn't know," said Mitch. "I just pretended." Mitch could feel his voice shaking. "And I didn't know that butterflies and birds and squirrels and woodchucks were wildlife. I lied to you, Molly, and I feel terrible."

There. He said it. He told Molly he had lied. Mitch felt better already.

Molly smiled. "It's okay, Mitch. I knew you didn't know. I could tell by your face."

"Why didn't you tell me you knew?" asked Mitch, feeling angry all over again.

"Because I remembered what Mom told you about Louis. She said God would help Louis learn to tell the truth." Molly giggled. "So I thought He could help you tell the truth too."

Mitch laughed. Molly was pretty neat. He liked having her for a sister, even if she did talk too much sometimes.

"Mitch," said Molly, "I was thinking maybe we could make a wildlife habitat in our backyard—like Rachel's. Her dad said there's a place we can write to for ideas. He said they even have pictures. Mom and Dad could help too.

"Rachel's dad said our houses are built right on the animals' nests. They got scared away. Isn't that terrible, Mitch? But they might come and visit us if we fix up our yard for them."

Mitch jumped up from the chair. "Wait a minute," he shouted. "I just got a great idea, Molly. I mean *you* just got a great idea. Maybe I could use it for the science fair."

"Use what?" asked Molly.

"Your idea about the wildlife habitat," said Mitch. He was so excited he started hopping around the room. "Maybe I could show kids how to make a wildlife habitat in their backyards. That would make a great science project."

"Wait till I tell Rachel," said Molly, giggling. "She helped you with your science project, and she didn't even know about it."

Mitch reached over and gave Molly a little hug. "*You* helped me, Molly, not Rachel."

Molly looked down at the floor. "Gee, thanks, Mitch," she said.

Mitch ran into the hall and leaned over the railing. "Dad, Mom, guess what?" shouted Mitch. "Molly gave me a great idea for my science project. I'm going to show everyone how to get butterflies and birds and woodchucks to visit their backyards. I'm going to call my project 'Backyard Visitors.' Rachel's dad knows how to do it."

"Well, you have been busy," said Mom.

"What a fine idea," said Dad.

Mitch and Molly told Mom and Dad what a backyard habitat is.

"Maybe we should take a look at our yard," said Dad.

Mitch and Molly and Mom and Dad went outside. In a few minutes Mitch knew just

where he would plant some honeysuckle. Dad found a place for the wood pile. Mother picked a branch on the oak tree for a bird feeder. And Molly phoned Rachel for the address of the National Wildlife Federation.

With Mom's help, Mitch wrote the federation a letter that night. He asked for their plan for a backyard habitat. Dad said he would mail it on his way to work the next day. Then Mitch and Molly said good-night to Mom and Dad.

Mitch climbed into bed and pulled his football pillow under his head.

He yawned and closed his eyes. He felt good inside. He and Molly were friends again. He had a great new idea for the science fair. He knew God had forgiven him for telling a lie. The pain in his stomach was gone. Thank you, God, Mitch prayed as he drifted off to sleep.

SOME THINGS YOU CAN DO TO SAVE GOD'S GREEN EARTH

Ask your teacher at school or Sunday school to plan a science fair like the one Mitch had at his school. Here are some ideas to suggest:

• Show how a bird feeder is built and what kind of food to leave out for different kinds of birds.

• Show how empty glass jars and bottles can be used again.

• Give a report on why it is important to recycle paper and glass.

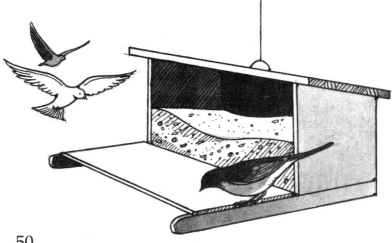

For more information about projects, write to the

National Wildlife Federation
Backyard Wildlife Habitat Program
1412 16th Street, NW
Washington, DC 20036

Mitch and Molly
And the Wild Surprise

Mitch ran through the entrance gate at the zoo. He felt his red T-shirt pull out of his shorts as he ran. "Mom, Dad, I want to see the monkeys first," shouted Mitch. "They're my favorite."

This was the day Mitch had waited for. Today he turned nine. He and his family were going to celebrate his birthday at the zoo.

Mitch could hear Molly running up behind him. Her Minnie Mouse sneakers squeaked as she ran. "I like monkeys too," she said. "It's funny the way they swing in the trees."

"Lead the way, Mitch," called Dad. "You know more about the zoo than we do."

"We'll follow you," said Mother. "But don't get too far ahead. We don't want to lose each other."

Mitch grabbed his sister by the hand and skipped down the path to the monkey exhibit. "There they are," shouted Mitch. "Look, Molly. See the ones hanging upside down by their tails. We saw them on our third-grade field trip."

"I can hang upside down on the monkey bars at the park," said Molly. "And Grandpa calls me his little monkey."

"Molly, that's just a nickname. These are *real* monkeys. They're called spider monkeys," said Mitch. "They're the only kind that can hang by their tails." Mitch ran up to the exhibit and leaned against the wall. "Look at the one with the tan fur," he said. "He's holding onto a branch with his arms and legs *and* tail. See, Molly? He looks like a giant spider."

"Is that why he's called a spider monkey?" asked Molly.

"That's right," said Mitch. "We learned about spider monkeys in school."

"I know," said Molly. "You did your report on them. And you read it to Mommy and Daddy and me at dinner. Remember? You showed us a picture too."

"Hey, that's right, I did," said Mitch. "See, they only have four fingers. Most other monkeys have four fingers and a thumb like we do."

Mitch watched Molly counting the fingers on the monkey closest to her. "Molly, look at this sign," he said. "It tells about spider monkeys. They like fruits and nuts, and they live high up in the trees."

Mitch pointed to the next sentence. "I don't know these words," he said. "Dad, come here." Mitch pulled his dad over to the sign on the exhibit. "Please read this part about the spider monkeys."

Dad put on his reading glasses. "Let's see," he said. "Spider monkeys live in the tropical forests of Central and South America. They are an endangered species."

"What does *endangered* mean?" asked Molly.

Mitch thought for a minute. Then he told Molly what he had learned in school. "It means there isn't enough room for them to live. And there's no place to have their babies, so they start to disappear," said Mitch. "Our teacher said some animals even become *extinct*. That means they die out and are gone from the earth forever."

"Like dinosaurs?" asked Molly.

"That's right," said Dad.

"That's terrible," said Molly, frowning. "How come there isn't enough room in the forest? I thought forests had lots of trees."

Mitch tucked his shirt into his shorts. "Well, some do," he said. "But the forests in South America are endangered. Mr. Bond said people cut down the trees to build houses and other buildings. And some people cut the trees for firewood."

"That's not fair," said Molly. "The spider monkeys live in those trees."

"You're right. It's not fair," said Dad.

"I wish I could have a spider monkey of my very own," said Mitch. "I wish I could have two of them. A boy and a girl. I'd take such good care of them. They'd be happy, and they'd have babies and they wouldn't be endangered."

"I feel the same way," said Mother. "I wish everyone would do at least one thing to keep God's earth green and safe for all creatures."

Mother pulled out a bottle of grape juice from a large bag. "How about cooling off with a drink?" she asked. "There are some benches under that tree. We can watch the monkeys from there."

Mitch and Molly and Mother and Dad sat down in the shade and drank their juice.

"Did you know there are other endangered animals too?" asked Dad

"Yeah. We learned that too," said Mitch. "Mr. Bond read us a report from the zoo. It said about 20 different kinds of endangered plants and animals become extinct every *week*!"

Dad collected the empty juice cups and put them back in Mother's bag. "That's amazing," he said. "I had no idea there were so many. I read that the panda bear, the rhinoceros, and the African elephant are also endangered," he said. "Even the hummingbird."

"The hummingbird?" Molly asked. "Daddy, that's terrible. Rachel has hummingbirds in her yard now. Does that mean they're going to die?"

Mitch interrupted before Dad could answer. "No, Molly. Those birds are safe because Rachel is helping them. She planted their favorite flowers in her yard, remember?"

"She made a little birdhouse for them too," said Molly.

"And she gives them fresh seed and water

every day," said Dad.

Molly jumped back and forth over a little curb next to the grass. "You mean if we help the animals they might not be endangered anymore?" asked Molly.

"That's right," said Mother. "People here at the zoo work with endangered animals, like the spider monkey. They give them a good place to live. They plant trees and build enclosures like the ones the animals have in nature."

"And the zookeepers feed the animals the right kind of food. They get healthy, and then they can have babies, right Mom?" asked Mitch.

"That's right," said Mother.

"Let's move on, shall we?" asked Dad. "We have a lot of animals to see today."

Mitch led Molly and Mother and Dad to the elephant enclosure. Mitch laughed at how the elephants picked up hay with their trunks. Molly said they smelled awful. She held her nose.

"Can we see the birds now?" asked Mother.

Mitch and Molly and Mother and Dad visited the bird exhibit. Then it was time for lunch. Mitch found a picnic table by the food stand. Dad said a prayer before they ate. "Thank You, God, for this good food, for this lovely day together. And we thank You especially for Mitch. Bless him on his birthday. Amen."

Mitch felt warm inside. Everyone in the family was looking at him and smiling. It was a good birthday.

After lunch, Mother and Dad took Mitch and Molly to the gift shop. "You may choose something for your birthday," said Dad. "What looks good to you?"

Mitch ran over to the book section. "Here's a book on spider monkeys," he said. "I'd like to get this."

Then he saw Molly walk over to a table with colorful T-shirts. "Hey, Mitch, look at this," she called. "Here's a shirt with two spider monkeys hanging upside down in a tree. Just like the ones we saw."

"That's neat," said Mitch. "Since I can't have my very own monkeys, I can get a book or a shirt about them." Mitch walked back and forth between the bookshelf and the shirt table. "Now I don't know which one to get."

"I have an idea," said Mother. "We'll buy you the book, and you can use this money from Grandma and Grandpa for the shirt." Mother pulled an envelope out of her purse. "Grandpa said to pick out something you'd really like."

"Wow!" Mitch didn't know what else to say. A book and a shirt about spider monkeys. He was sure they were the next best thing to a real monkey. "Thanks, Mom and Dad and Molly. I'll call Grandma and Grandpa when I get home." Mitch picked up the book and shirt. He waited while Dad paid the lady behind the counter.

Mitch and Molly and Mom and Dad walked out of the gift shop. Dad looked at his watch. "Nearly time to go home," he said. "But it seems to me we forgot one important thing.

Can anyone remember what that is?"

Molly giggled. "I can. I can," she shouted.

Mitch wondered what all the giggling was about.

Mother put her arm around Mitch's shoulder. "Well, birthday boy," she said. "We have one more surprise, don't we Molly? Do you want to give it to Mitch?"

"Yes, I do," said Molly, hopping from one foot to the other.

Mother reached into her purse and pulled out a large envelope. Mitch's name was on the front in gold letters. Molly handed it to Mitch. She jumped up and down and clapped her hands while Mitch opened it. Inside was a certificate from the director of the zoo. Mitch read it out loud.

Welcome to Our Family

Thank you for joining our
Adopt-an-Animal Program.
Your gift of $50 will help take care
of spider monkeys for one year.
You are helping us save
endangered animals.

The certificate was signed by the director of the zoo. And with the certificate was a colored picture of a spider monkey hanging upside down in a tree.

Mitch felt his eyes get watery. And he could feel his heart pound. "Is adopting an animal like adopting a person?" asked Mitch.

"Something like that," said Dad. "The animals stay in the zoo, of course. But the money we paid will help give them extra–good care. And you can come and visit them whenever you want to. You can think of them as your own pets, if you want to."

"Wow!" Mitch could hardly believe it. What a birthday. It was even better than he wished for. He had a book and a new shirt about spider monkeys. And he was an adoptive parent too!

Mitch hugged Mother and Dad and Molly. "Thanks," he said. "This is the best birthday ever."

SOMETHING YOU CAN DO TO SAVE GOD'S GREEN EARTH

Call a zoo near your home and ask about their animal adoption program. Your family, classroom, or Sunday school class could collect money to adopt an endangered animal. If you do not have a zoo near you, write for more information to

The American Association
of Zoological Parks and Aquariums
4550 Montgomery Ave., Suite 940 N
Bethesda, MD 20814

Mitch and Molly
And the Cleanup Crew

Molly waved a sheet of white paper in front of Mitch's face. "Look what I made for Daddy's birthday present," she said.

Mitch looked at the picture of Molly and Dad pasted inside a heart on the paper. Molly's not a very good artist, thought Mitch. But she's only in kindergarten. The words on the bottom of the paper said, "Happy Birthday, Daddy. Love, Molly."

"Wow, Molly. That's neat. Did you make it all by yourself?"

Molly smiled proudly. "Yes, I did," she said. "Mom said we're going to have a party for Dad tomorrow." Molly spun around while she talked. "I'm going to give it to him then. Grandma and Grandpa are coming, and so are Nick and Nancy, and Aunt Laura and Uncle Rob."

"Tomorrow? What time?" asked Mitch. "Tomorrow we're having a kids' cleanup crew at church. We can't have the party tomorrow. It's not fair. I'll miss the contest." Mitch pounded his football pillow and stamped his feet.

"Gosh, Mitch," said Molly. "You're not very nice. It's Daddy's birthday. You *have* to be here."

Mitch dashed down the stairs. "Mom, Mom, where are you? It's important."

"In the den, Mitch," she called. "What's all the fuss?"

"I didn't know you were having a party for Dad tomorrow. You can't, Mom. Tomorrow's the cleanup crew at church. All the Sunday school kids are helping. We're going to clean up the church and the grass and the play-ground. And we're going to plant flowers and mow the lawn and pick up the leaves. I want to help, Mom, please!"

Mitch couldn't stand still. He hopped from one foot to the other while he talked. He was almost out of breath.

"Mitch, settle down. I haven't forgotten," said Mother. "The cleanup crew starts at 10:00, and the party starts at 11:30. You can go to church from 10:00 to 12:00 and still be home on time for lunch and birthday cake. How does that sound?"

"You don't understand," said Mitch. "Mrs. Garcia said there will be a prize for the kid who brings the most helpers." Mitch put his arms around his mother's neck. "Pretty please, Mom. Couldn't we have Dad's party another day? I wanted you and Dad and Molly to be my helpers."

Mother turned and gave Mitch a hug. "I know you're disappointed. But the party is already planned. We can't change it now. I don't remember hearing about the helpers or the prize. Did you tell me that before?"

"I forgot to bring home the note," said Mitch.

"I'm sorry, Mitch. But I want you home for Daddy's party. Cheer up. You can still be part of the cleanup crew before the party starts."

"I know," said Mitch. "But Mrs. Garcia said this would be a good way to tell other people about how to keep God's earth green and clean. It won't be fun without taking helpers."

Mother patted Mitch on the shoulder. "I'm sorry," she said. "Maybe we can have our own cleanup crew right here at home. Would you like that?"

"Sure," said Mitch in a low voice. He kicked at the carpet as he walked outside.

Molly was bouncing a ball against the garage door. "Gosh, Molly, I goofed again," said Mitch. "It's my fault for not telling Mom about the prize and the helpers."

Molly looked sad, but she didn't say anything.

That night Mitch went to bed thinking about the cleanup crew. Then he thought about his dad. He wished he could feel happy. He didn't want to spoil his dad's birthday party.

The next morning Mitch walked into the family room. Dad was reading the paper. Fluffy was sleeping in a sunny spot on the rug like she always did. Mother and Molly were hanging paper decorations on the light over the table. "Happy birthday, Dad," said Mitch.

"Thanks, Mitch. So far it's very happy," said Dad smiling.

At 10 minutes to 10:00, Mother drove Mitch to the church grounds. "I'll pick you up at 12:00 sharp," said Mother. "Wait for me under the pine tree."

Mitch waved good-bye to his mother.

Then he ran to the playground. Mrs. Garcia was passing out trash bags and rakes, paintbrushes and buckets.

Mitch saw mothers and fathers and sisters and brothers standing in a circle. There was even a grandma with gray hair holding a can of paint. He wished he wasn't all by himself. He wished his mom and dad and Molly could join the cleanup crew with him. Or maybe he could have asked Grandma and Grandpa to come.

"Let's get started," said Mrs. Garcia. Mitch walked over to the flower bed in front of the church. He picked the dead leaves and buds off the plants. And he picked up bits of paper that had blown in from the street.

Then he saw something shiny under the pine tree. Mitch ran to see what it was. Soda cans! Someone had dropped their soda pop cans under the tree. Mitch put them in his bag.

Mitch watched his friend Matt sweep pine needles off the driveway. Matt's sister, Jenny, washed down the picnic tables in the kids' playground. This is fun, thought Mitch. When everyone helps it goes fast.

Mitch waved to his friend Matt. Wow! thought Mitch. He has five helpers. He's going to win.

Mitch saw Matt's mom planting marigolds around the Sunday school building. His dad was fixing a loose window. His big sister and brother were carrying trash bags out to the street. And his cousin was nailing some loose boards on the picnic table.

Mitch looked at his watch. It was almost 12:00. He had to meet his mother under the pine tree at 12:00 sharp. Mitch walked over to Mrs. Garcia and gave her the bag and tools. "Today's my dad's birthday," said Mitch. "I have to go now. We're having a party."

Mrs. Garcia put her hands on Mitch's shoulders and smiled. "Thanks for being part of the cleanup crew," she said. "You did a great job."

Mitch said good-bye to Mrs. Garcia and to Matt and Peter and his other friends. Then he started walking toward the pine tree. Suddenly Mitch saw Molly running toward him. And behind Molly were Mom and Dad, and Grandpa and Grandma, and Nick and Nancy, and Aunt Laura and Uncle Rob.

"What are you doing here?" shouted Mitch. "Am I late?"

"No, we're the ones who are late," called Dad as he ran up to Mitch. "Molly told me about the cleanup crew and the prize for the most helpers," said Dad. "So I decided to have my birthday party up here."

Dad turned to Mom and Molly and Grandpa and Grandma and the others. "We all agreed it was a great idea, so here we are. We want to be part of the cleanup crew."

"Wow!" Mitch didn't know what else to say. His eyes got watery. For a second Mitch thought he was going to cry. "Gee, thanks Dad," said Mitch. "Thanks, Molly." Mitch looked at everyone in his family. They were all smiling at him.

"Will you show me what to do?" asked Molly.

"Sure," said Mitch.

"Let's get started," said Grandpa. He winked at Mitch and Molly. "The sooner we finish, the sooner we can have some of those great cupcakes your mother made."

Just then Mrs. Garcia blew her whistle. "Time for lunch, everyone. We'll start again in 30 minutes."

"Perfect timing," said Dad. "Let's have our picnic under that tree."

Mitch could hardly believe it. Mother had packed a big basket with all the party food. There were tuna sandwiches and milk and carrot sticks and chips and his favorite cupcakes. She even brought little candles to put in the cupcakes.

"Mom brought enough cupcakes for everyone on the team," said Molly.

"You did?" asked Mitch. "That's neat."

After lunch Mother passed out the cupcakes

and the candles. All the people on the cleanup crew sang "Happy Birthday" to Mitch's dad. Mitch felt so happy he thought he would burst.

Mrs. Garcia blew her whistle again and everyone went back to work. Mitch and Molly and Nick and Nancy helped clean out the tool shed. Then Mitch saw Grandma and Grandpa washing the cupboards in the church kitchen.

Mom and Dad waved as they walked by. They had a sack of clothes from the lost-and-found closet. Mitch saw Molly help them put the clothes in boxes for families at the homeless shelter. Aunt Laura and Uncle Rob asked Mitch to help them plant two little trees in the children's playground.

At the end of the day, Mitch was tired and dirty. But he was happy too. He looked at the church and the Sunday school building and the playground. They were clean and green. He was proud to be part of the cleanup crew.

At 3:00 Mrs. Garcia blew her whistle again. "Everyone," she shouted, "Get in a big circle.

Let's pray. Then I have an announcement."

Mitch and his family joined hands in the big circle. "Heavenly Father," said Mrs. Garcia, "thank You for our church and for our church family. Thank You for Your green earth. And thank You for all these people who worked so hard today. May You receive all the glory. We pray in Jesus' name. Amen."

Then Mrs. Garcia took a deep breath. Everyone waited to see what she was going to do next. "Now is the time we've all been waiting for," she said, smiling. "It's time to give the prize to the person who brought the most helpers."

Mitch looked at Matt. Matt looked back.

"This year the prize goes to Mitch. He had *nine* helpers. Let's all clap for Mitch and his family. Thanks to all of you," she said.

"Nine helpers?" said Mitch out loud. "Wow! I didn't know I had that many." Mitch counted heads. "There were Molly and Mom and Dad and Grandma and Grandpa and Nick

and Nancy and Aunt Laura and Uncle Rob."
Nine helpers, Mitch thought. He felt his eyes
get watery again.

Mrs. Garcia put her arm around Mitch.
Then she led him into the middle of the circle.
"Mitch," she said, "I'd like to present you with this
little fig tree. Thank you for helping keep God's
earth green. And thank you for sharing your
family with us."

A fig tree, Mitch thought. He remembered
Jesus talking about fig trees in the Bible.

Everyone stared at him and smiled. They
clapped again. Mitch felt warm inside. He looked
at his father. "I'm going to give my tree a name,"
he said.

"What's that?" asked Dad.

"I'm going to call it the Happy Birthday
tree."

Dad hugged Mitch. Mitch hugged Dad
back. Mitch knew it had been a happy day for
everyone.

SOMETHING YOU CAN DO TO SAVE GOD'S GREEN EARTH

Ask your pastor or Sunday school teacher if students can set up a cleanup crew at your church. Ask parents to help too. Everyone can do something to make the buildings and the grounds look clean and green. You can have a cleanup crew at your house too. Maybe your family could invite people to help, and then serve a picnic lunch afterwards.